D0174509

Foxy Fox

Barbara deRubertis
Illustrated by Eva Vagreti Cockrille

The Kane Press
New York

Cover Design: Sheryl Kagen

Library of Congress Catalog Card Number: 96-75014

ISBN 1-57565-003-7

10 9 8 7 6 5

First published in the United States of America in 1997 by The Kane Press.
Printed in China.

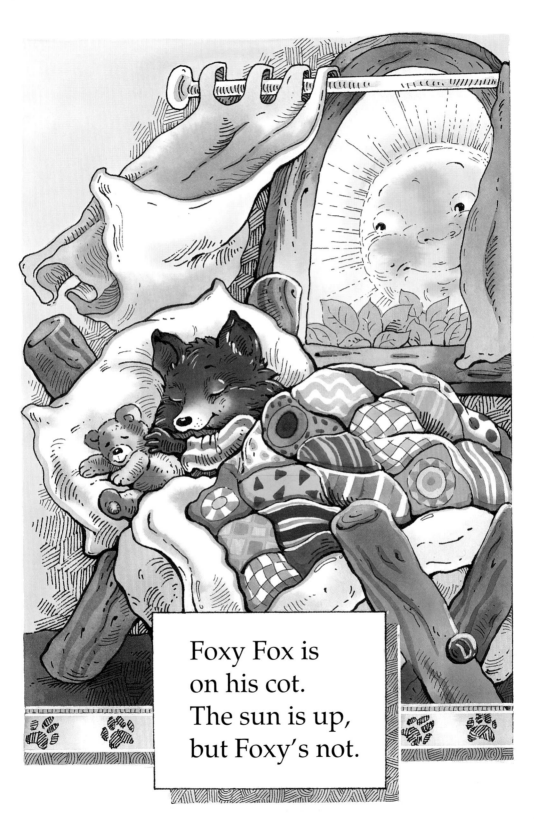

Foxy Fox is
on his cot.
The sun is up,
but Foxy's not.

"Tick, tock,"
says the clock.
"Tick, tock.
Tick, tock."

"BONG, BONG,"
says the clock.

BONG!
BONG!

Foxy Fox
bops the clock.

"I have to hop down
to the shop.
I have to mop for
Mom and Pop."

But Foxy does not
feel like hopping.
Foxy does not
feel like mopping.

9

"Were you lost?"
says Mom Fox.
"It's time to mop!"
says Pop Fox.

Mom says, "When you stop the mopping, you can help me with the chopping."

11

Foxy flops and slops the mop.

Pop says, "No, no, Foxy! Stop!"

Foxy chops and
chops and chops.
Foxy drops and
drops and drops.

Mom says, "Foxy drops a lot! Foxy even drops the pot!"

Pop says, "Foxy,
you must stop!
Or you can't help us
in the shop!"

"I can help you,
Mom and Pop.
I can help you
in the shop."

"One more chance!"
says Mom Fox.
"One more chance!"
says Pop Fox.

Mom and Pop
look at the clock.
"We must hurry
down the block.

"We must go
pick up a box—
a box of socks
for Grandpa Fox."

Foxy hops around the shop. "I can mop and I can chop!

"I am not a
slobby slob.
I can do a
GOOD job.

"I can pour,

and I can plop.

"I can flip,

and I can flop."

Foxy frosts,

and Foxy tosses.

28

"I will have two
happy bosses!"

What a shock
for Mom and Pop!

30

"Foxy Fox,
    you are the TOPS!"